I'm Sorry

For Dylan and Megan

I'm Sorry

Text copyright © 2000 by Sam McBratney

Illustrations copyright © 2000 by Jennifer Eachus

Manufactured in China. All rights reserved. No part of this book may be used or reproduced in any manner whatsoever without written permission except in the case of brief quotations embodied in critical articles and reviews. For information address HarperCollins Children's Books, a division of HarperCollins Publishers, 195 Broadway, New York, NY 10007.

www.harperchildrens.com

Library of Congress Cataloging-in-Publication Data

McBratney, Sam.

I'm sorry / Sam McBratney ; illustrations by Jennifer Eachus.

p. cm.

1st American ed.

Eachus, Jennifer, ill.

ISBN-10: 0-06-028686-5 (trade bdg.) — ISBN-13: 978-0-06-028686-6 (trade bdg.)

ISBN-10: 0-06-079927-7 (pbk.) — ISBN-13: 978-0-06-079927-4 (pbk.)

[1. Friendship—Fiction. 2. Apologizing—Fiction.] I. McBratney, Sam II. Title.

PZ7.M1218 Im 2000   99060933

[E]—dc21   CIP

                                                                                                 AC

Frist published in the United Kingdom by HarperCollins Publishers Ltd., 2000

14 SCP 10 9 8 7 6

I'm Sorry

Sam McBratney

Illustrations by Jennifer Eachus

HarperCollinsPublishers

I have a friend I love the best.

She plays at my house every day,
or else I play at hers.

I have a friend I love the best.
I think she's nice.

The things we do
always make me laugh,
and she thinks I'm nice, too.

She lets me be the teacher
when we teach our
toys to read . . .

. . . I let her be the doctor
and fix my broken bones.

We make her baby smile
when he wakes up from his nap . . .

. . . and sometimes
we put our rain boots
on

to see how deep
the puddles are.

I have a friend I love the best.
I think she's nice,

and she thinks I'm nice, too.
The things we do always make me laugh.
But . . .

I SHOUTED at my friend today,

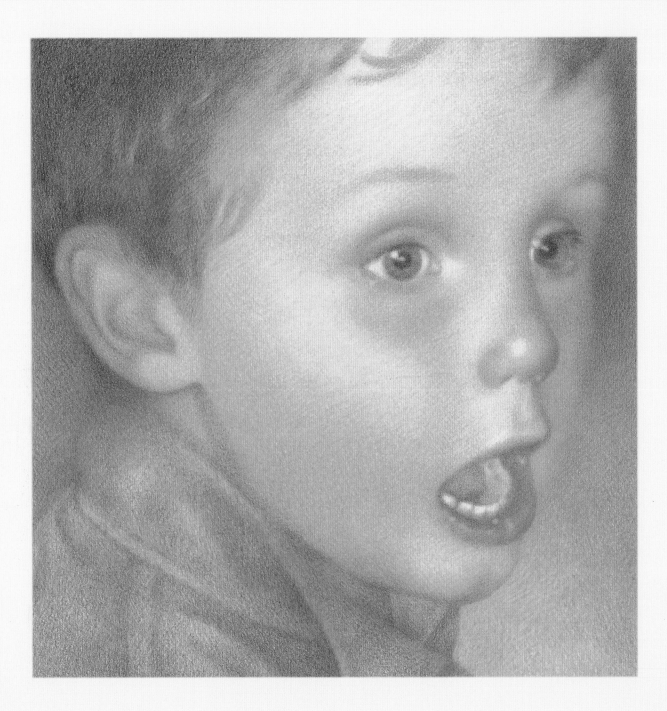

and she SHOUTED back at me.

I wouldn't speak to
her anymore, and she
wouldn't speak to me.

My friend shouted at me today,
and I shouted back at her.

She won't play with me anymore,
and I won't play with her.

I pretend my friend's not there,

and she pretends she doesn't care, but . . .

I do care.

If my friend were as
sad as I am sad, this
is what she would do:

She would come and say, "I'm sorry,"

and I would say sorry, too.